"SAY YOUR PRAYERS, PREACHER BOY"

"Let's do it!"

Rodney L. Baumberger

authorHOUSE®

AuthorHouse™
1663 Liberty Drive
Bloomington, IN 47403
www.authorhouse.com
Phone: 1-800-839-8640

First published by AuthorHouse 11/24/2009

ISBN: 978-1-4490-5082-5 (e)
ISBN: 978-1-4490-5081-8 (sc)

Library of Congress Control Number: 2009912149

Printed in the United States of America
Bloomington, Indiana

This book is printed on acid-free paper.

CHAPTER ONE

"Say your prayers, Preacher Boy!" said the pimply faced, longhaired chunk of meaness. "I'm going to hit you so hard, you'll be doing snow angels on the ground!" Someone in the crowd around the two boys laughed aloud at the mental image that the bully's words provoked.

Fil, who was the unwilling center of attention, grimaced. He felt the crowd shifting in closer, not one of them wanting to miss a verbal barb or a thrown punch. They wanted blood and Fil knew whose blood they wanted. He looked around for a friendly or even a sympathetic face, but didn't see anything but blood lust. His best friend, Joe, was here when this started, but had evidently left when he saw what was about to occur.

Fil turned his attention back to the hulking young man who was now flexing his big biceps. His nose picked up the stink of rancid perspiration from the grease ball in front of him.

The big bully's name was Link Smith to his face, Stink behind his back. He was a lot bigger than Fil. He had to go six feet, two hundred pounds, at least. That was three inches and thirty pounds difference between the two.

"C'mon Link, I don't want any trouble." said Fil, " You know you can beat me up, so let's just forget it." Link snorted through his nose, "maybe I just want to know what your face feels like on my fists!" he grinned and looked around the close pressed crowd hoping for a favorable response for his clever wit.

Fil sighed. This whole thing started at lunch earlier. Two more days and school would have been through for the summer and he wouldn't be in the fix he was in now. He had picked up his tray and wended his way through the food line, picking out a healthful variety of the different types of fare, before going over to sit with his friend Joe. Sitting down, he folded his hands and asked the Lord's blessing for what he was about to eat. Fil could feel the eyes on him as he bowed his head. Being a newly saved Christian, he was still self-conscious of the way people gawked when he showed his faith in prayer.

It had been the greatest feeling in the world when he became born again and he refused to be embarrassed when some of the other students snickered and pointed at him when he thanked God.

The troubled started when he had finished his prayer and noticed a shadow crossing the table from behind. The accompanying smell told him who it was before a meaty hand slapped him in the back of the head.

" Hey Hooper!" Link snickered, "wake up!" Fil's head was driven forward and tears came into his eyes, not so much from the pain inflicted, but the embarrassment of so many people enjoying his predicament.

"Jerk!" muttered Joe under his breath. Smith, who was walking away, instantly whirled around and in one giant step was back at Fil's side hovering menacing over him.

"What did you say?" he demanded. Fil glanced at Joe, anger in his eyes, before he slid sideways in his chair angling towards Link.

"I didn't say anything to you." He said truthfully. "Then it must have been your buddy," Link shifted his steely gaze towards Joe. "How about it Ryan? Got enough guts to say it out loud?"

Joe fidgeted fearfully in his seat, his eyes averted from Link. The bully reached for Joe's shirtfront and grabbed it tight, popping buttons and forcefully lifted him from the seat. "I'm talking to you, punk!"

Joe dangled from Link's fist as he tried to sputter out an answer."I...I didn't sa... say anything!' he stammered. Link shoved the much smaller boy back into his seat, clattering the back of the plastic chair against the table.

"Then it must have been you Preacher boy." He looked around the silent cafeteria, "I thought good Christians didn't lie." He stared down at Fil, "tell you what, Preacher boy. I'll meet you in the parking lot after school and I'll beat the devil out of you. That way you won't be tempted to lie again." He had laughed and turned away striding confidently across the floor. As he left the room, everyone let out a sigh of relief, glad that Fil had been the target, not them.

3

Fil had rounded on Joe ready to give him a verbal thrashing but stopped when he saw tears coursing down his best friends face. "I'm sorry, real sorry Fil." He mumbled. He stood up from the table and leaving his tray full of food, he walked quickly away.

Joe hesitated, started to get up, and then turned back to his lunch. Everyone was still watching him and he was not going to show fear. Still, He said a silent prayer to God to help him out of this mess. As he ate, he decided to leave it in His hands.

Three o'clock came and Fil had met Joe after their last class walking towards Fil's old Chevy impala. It wasn't much of a car, a 66, but it was all he could afford on his part time job. Lord knows, his mother and father couldn't afford to buy him a car and he wouldn't have asked them. He took pride in being his own man.

As he approached the car, his heart dropped. Leaning on the hood was Link and in the back ground he could see a group of students moving quickly forward. They didn't want to miss the blood letting.

"Oh great!" Fil muttered under his breath," Just what I need!" He thought briefly about going back into the school as if he forgotten something, but he realized with two full days of school left, he didn't think he could avoid his fate.

Let's not go over, Fil," Joe said. "Let's go get a teacher or someone." Mirroring Fil's thoughts. "No, that's not going to work. Fil disagreed softly. "Maybe an apology will prevent this from happening. After all didn't

4

Proverbs 15:1 say, " A soft answer turns away wrath, but a harsh word stirs up anger?"

"It might have, I don't know, but I do know that Link Smith is there with his pals and I don't want to be here!" said Joe. "C'mon Fil, let's get out of here. There's only two more days of school, we can stay away from him.' He pleaded.

"Nope!" Grunted Fil, "we're going to stop it right now." Reflecting back, he realized that was the last he seen of Joe. Now he was the main attraction to a massacre. "Soft words…soft words… the mantra echoed in his mind. "Wait a minute Link." Fil said, eyes on the bullies big hands, "I mean it. I don't want to fight you. I'd rather be your friend."

Instantly suspicious, eyes narrowing, Link hesitated. " What did you say?" He asked unbelievingly.

"Really Link, I want to be your friend." Fil waited, hands at his side, waiting for the bullies reaction.

Link seemed to think over the words for a brief moment, then without any preamble, struck.

The big right hand came from out of nowhere, yet seemed to come forward in excruciating slow motion. Fil was able to see the black hair that covered the joints below the knuckles and noted idiotically that there was a small scar, shaped like a crescent moon, on the index finger's knuckle. Then the world turned into a kaleidoscope of bright colors as he was twisted around in a circle from the force of the blow.

"Ohs" and "Ahs" were the prevalent sounds from the spectators as he ended the spin on his hands and knees. Looking at the pavement through slitted eyes, he marveled at the bright specks of mica that caught the strong rays of the mid afternoon's sun. His wonderment turned to groggy concern when a fat red drop of blood splattered down from his face to dull some of the miniature sun bursts from the reflective mineral.

Slowly, he raised his head up towards his tormentor. He gasped, when again in slow motion, he saw the big work boot being drawn back. He tried to make his numb body obey his command and roll out of the way, but his brain was short circuited and refused to issue the proper orders.

Surreally, the slow motion of the boot turned into the blinding speed of a meteorite flashing across the horizon and was instantly speeding it's way into Fil's exposed side. The strength of Link Smith became very apparent when the force of the kick "Whumpped" Fil Hooper upwards into a shape reminiscent of an inchworm measuring a leaf.

His face was skinned back and he could feel the harshness of the pavement chipping into his teeth as he slammed back down. Even with his eyes closed he knew that the punishment would not be over yet. He tensed up and took another ferocious blow to the side. In a far off distance, he heard disconnected words and sounds that told him of the primal excitement of the surrounding on lookers. Dimly, far off, he heard the wail of a siren pulling closer, mercifully, the blows stopped as some of the on lookers fled the scene.

6

"What's going on here?" A gruff voice growled to the remaining spectators. They looked furtively at each other, but no one would volunteer a single word. Whether from shame or fear of retribution from "Stink," they kept their mouth shut.

The uniformed cop cleared the crowd back, and then kneeled beside the bloodied Fil. "What happened here son?" Which one did this?"

Everyone waited with bated breath. Would the goody two-shoe Christian blow big Link Smith in, assuming himself a measure of safety for the last two days of school, or would he do as his God commanded him in Matthew 5:39 and turn the other cheek?

They waited as Fil sat up and wiped the blood from his face with the hankie pulled surreptitiously from his back pocket. They waited as he blew his nose, then rose unsteadily to his feet, putting his hankie in his back pocket as he leaned against the hood of his

Impala, much as Smith had done earlier.

"Well son?" Asked the cop again. "Who did this to you?" Fil looked Link in the eye. What was there? Surely not fear of the situation. Fil knew that Link had been in trouble a number of occasions and this was just another speed bump in his road to being a grade-A, numero uno reprobate.

Fil had been serious when he had told Link he wanted to be his friend. It kind of surprised him when he had made the offer. The words had come unbidden, but it had seemed right when he heard himself speak. He hadn't enlightened Link to the fact that it had been Joe that called him a jerk, and neither would he inform the policeman who caused his injuries. He knew he would be lectured and maybe even threatened by an angry law official if he denied the facts of the situation, but so be it.

"I fell." Was all he would say.

"Aw, come on now!" snarled the cop. "I'm not stupid." He pointed a fat finger to Smith. "You think you're gaining something by helping this hard case?" He leaned closer to Fil. "He's beaten up more kids then you can count and you're trying to help him out? Oh C'mon kid, do you think you'll be the last? Just say the word, I'll take it from there."

Fil simply shook his head from side to side, ignoring the lancet of pain that caused him to wince slightly. "Alright then." The cop looked at the remaining spectators. "Anyone here want to tell me what really happened?" No one moved, no one said a word. Disgusted, the policeman shook his head. "Alright then, break it up! Get out of here before I run you all in!"

Fil watched the crowd climbing into their vehicles and leaving by foot. He was aware of the close scrutiny he was receiving from the upset official. Still, he never uttered a word and kept the pain inside. He was very interested in watching the kids leaving in their automobiles and was hoping the cop would take the hint and leave. Yeah right.

"You're stupid kid." The cop's fetid breath washed across Fil's nose. It took total concentration not to gag. "I've seen hundreds of punks like that Smith kid. The jails are full of them. One of these days he is going to go too far and cripple or kill someone." The officer eyeballed Fil balefully. "When that happens, I think I will personally come to tell you that you could of stopped this idiot today. From here on out, any damage he does is your fault." He waited for a response from Fil. Not getting one he sighed heavily. "Gimme some I.D. kid."

Fil reached for his wallet, moving slowly as not to aggravate his sore ribs, he flipped through the transparent picture holders until he came to his driver's license. He slid it from the holder and handed it to the policeman.

The cop stared at it as if memorizing every detail. "Fil Hooper, 16 years old." The cop looked up. "Well, Fil Hooper, are you sure you don't want to tell me the truth?" Before Fil could answer, another voice interrupted them.

"What's going on here?"

The fat policeman and Fil turned to look at the new arrivals. It was the Principal of the school and his buddy Joe.

"I asked a question." Said the nattily clothed Mr. Sherman. The cop handed Fil his license and turned to the principal. "Just helping the boy from a nasty fall." He said sarcastically. Looking at Fil, "remember what I said. I'll be seeing you, I'm sure."

He waddled over to the flashing squad car and doused the revolving overhead lights. Without another look, he spun out of the now empty student parking lot.

"Joe said there was trouble out here, Mr. Hooper." He looked Fil up and down noting the cut oozing blood on the left cheekbone and the tattered knees of his jeans. "Want to tell me about it?"

"There's nothing to tell, Mr. Sherman." Fil stared into the principal's eyes. "Nothing at all."

Mr. Sherman held Fil's gaze for a long moment and then decided quickly that with only two more school days left that this incident could be expediently ignored since it was obvious that Hooper was willing to forget it. "I'll make a notation of this, Mr. Hooper and hopefully it will go away before next year." He turned and walked away, grateful he didn't have to complicate his remaining hours of school dealing with adolescent behavior.

Fil and Joe watched him leave before Joe turned to Fil. "Sorry I left you like that. I thought we needed help."

Fil snorted through his nose. "Not we, me!" He exclaimed sharply. "I'm the one bleeding because your mouth."

Joe dropped his head. "Yeah, you're right." He kicked a pebble, causing it to skitter across the paving. "You know what, Fil?" He said," I'm tired of being pushed around. I'm tired of being afraid of someone because they're bigger or stronger or meaner then me. I'm tired of it!" He repeated.

"So am I, but what can we do about it?" Track is over until next year." Fil cracked a small joke trying to ease his friend's torment.

Joe wouldn't look at Fil, keeping his eyes downcast. He rubbed his chin with his left hand and slipped his other hand into his jeans pocket before he said what was on his mind. "Karate."

Fil glanced sharply at Joe, "Karate?" He asked. "Yeah!" He met Fil's eyes, "I've been thinking about it for a couple of weeks and today has made up my mind." Joe took a deep breath. "I'm going to go check out some of the schools around here. "Interested?"

"Schools?" The question raced through Fil's mind. How many schools could be in

an area like this?"

Not that Claytown was small; it was a nice size community. Fil didn't know for sure, but he thought he heard his father say its population was around five thousand people.

Claytown was built around a small river and spilled over on both sides of its banks. Three bridges connected the town. All in all, it was a friendly place to live and raise your family.

Fil and his parents had moved here three years ago and He was still learning the different places and shops. He had never seen any Karate Schools and was curious as to where they were.

"I've never seen any schools around here. Where are they?" He asked.

"There's one outside of Claytown. It's called Brown's Karate. Then there are three other ones up north." U p north meant a fifteen-minute drive to Sales, a town twice the size of Claytown.

"Geez Joe, you're really serious about this, aren't you?

"Darn right I am." Joe's face turned serious as he slipped his other hand in his pocket and slightly hunched his shoulders. "I'm going to start checking them out tonight, want to go?" He asked.

Well yeah, but you know I have to clear it with mom and dad first." Fil frowned, "Mom won't care, she thinks I ought to be doing more activities anyway, but I don't know how Dad will re-act."

Joe snorted out a short laugh. "Tell him what happened today. He'll let you do it for sure."

"No Joe, that doesn't cut it with dad. You know he's a devout Christian and doesn't believe in violence or revenge." He thought, his right hand straying to his mouth cupping his lower jaw, and then smiled. "I'll talk to him tonight." He said.

"Call me later, see you Fil." Joe turned to walk away.

"Hey don't you want a ride?" Asked Fil.

"No thanks, I'll walk." Said Joe. "I need to think about what happened today."

"Gee, don't worry about it," said Fil, :I'm the one who was thrashed!"

"I know. That's what I have to think about. It should have been me." He walked away, adjusting his shirt to stay together by tucking the tail deep into his jeans so the missing buttons would be less noticeable.

Fil opened the door of his '66 chevy and slid behind the wheel. He positioned the rear view mirror towards him and reviewed his banged up face. He reached up and slightly pinched the cut on his cheekbone. It hurt, but not badly. He opened his mouth wide and checked out his teeth. None broken. Pulling up his shirt, he could see a nasty bruise welting up, but he pushed on each rib and although sore he didn't think there were any broke, cracked or sprung.

He was lucky that fat cop had shown up when he did. Another kick or two and he wouldn't of finished the school year out.

Karate, huh?" He mused out loud.

He repositioned the rear view mirror and drove to the local retail store where he worked in the storeroom.

CHAPTER TWO

Later that afternoon, Fil finished his shower and thundered down the steps to the television room. His dad was kicked back in his recliner reading the local paper. He always kept up with the news whether it was local events or situations occurring throughout the world. "Always remember Fil, knowledge is power," was one of his pet advices.

Dad, I need to talk to you." He said.

Carl Hooper put the paper aside and looked curiously at his son. He noticed the small laceration on his cheek and noticed his son was quietly excited.

"Okay son, talk to me."

"Joe and I were discussing Karate today…" Fil hesitated trying to read his father over that simple statement. "We want to check some schools out tonight."

Carl didn't day anything for a moment. "Does this have anything to do with the cut on you cheek?" He asked.

"Some of it, but not all." Fil replied. "I want to learn to defend myself."

"I see." Said Carl. "Tell me what happened today." After a simple explanation, Fil leaned back in his chair and waited.

"If you would have known Karate today, how would it have changed the outcome?" Carl asked.

"I wouldn't have been thumped on. I could of defended myself." Fil was thoughtful for a long moment. "There might not even had been a fight, if I would have had the knowledge to prevent it."

Carl marveled at the insight his son had shown. "Alright Fil, but I want to ask you one question before you go. Did you go to the Lord in prayer about this?"

"Yes sir, I did." Fil said quietly.

"You don't think a martial art with eastern origins would be against the teachings of our Lord?"

"No sir. I do not want to be a Buddhist or to embrace their religions. I want the physical and mental aspects of the sport, not the spiritual end."

"You have my permission to scout the schools out but..." Carl leaned forward and stared deep into Fil's eyes. "You need to get my permission to sign up."

"No problem, dad." Fil jumped up and headed to the phone to call Joe. "Thanks a lot, dad."

CHAPTER THREE

Joe and Fil rode in silence during the fifteen minutes it took to get to the city of Sales. Joe knew where the Karate schools were located and gave Fil the directions.

Joe had investigated a school earlier in the day and knew class started at seven o'clock. They wanted to be a little early so the could see the students go in.

Fil pulled into the graveled lot and parked. He looked at Joe and grinned. "Ready to go in, Joe?" He asked.

Joe answered Fil's grin with one of his own. "Look at me, Fil. I'm nervous and sweaty." His grin became a frown. "This is what I'm talking about, Fil. I want to have the confidence to go anywhere and do anything I want to do without feeling like a scared little boy!"

"I'm nervous too," said Fil, "let's go in." They exited the Impala and walked over to the heavy glass door. They could see inside the building and was able to see some of the students on the floor stretching out.

Fil opened the door and entered first, holding the door so Joe could follow. They stood in a waiting area that featured a worn couch and chair book ended by end tables laded with old issues of Black Belt magazines.

Some of the students inside the carpeted area gazed curiously at them, but did not make an attempt to show any kind of welcome. Fil felt a little out of place, but was determined to see it through.

"Can I help you?" cracked a voice from inside a small office that opened to their right.

"Uh…yeah!" answered Fil. We're kind of interested in taking karate. We thought we would check your school out."

The man rose and came from behind a battered black and strode confidently from the office.

"This is the place to come. We are the best! No one is any better then me." He extended a hand to Fil. "My name is Cain, Mr. Cain." He than shook hands with Joe. "Hang on a second, I need to get the class started." He turned to go into the workout area bowing from the waist before entering the open space. "Line up!" He bellowed and watched closely as his students sprang to attention in a straight line before him. "Yes sir!" They shouted.

They looked splendecent in their white karate outfits garnished with different colored belts.

"Face the flags and bow." In unison they snapped out a quick bow. "Face here and bow to me!" He bellowed again. The students did as instructed.

"You!" Mr. Cain pointed to a student at the beginning of the line to his left. "Stretch'em out."

"Yes Sir" the young man said. Again he bowed to Cain.

"Come with me." Cain motioned them to the office. He had them into his office and pointed to two chairs facing the battered desk.

"Sit down." He ordered.

Fil and Joe sat. Mr. Cain shifted around to an old filing cabinet and started to rifle through it.

Fil used the moment to look around the office. What He saw impressed him. Certificates galore hung from the wall behind the busy Karate teacher. There must have been fifteen colorful framed parchments. The most prominent one proclaimed Dean A. Cain a 7th Dan Master of the martial arts. While Fil was duly impressed with these, what really drew both his and Joe's attention, was the wall of trophies. From the floor to the ceiling the walls shelving was tightly packed with golden figures frozen in a flying side kick. After closer scrutiny, he realized that almost everyone was a first place award.

"Wow!" Thought Fil, "I want one of those!"

Mr. Cain pulled four sheets of paper from the filing cabinet and turned to face Fil and Joe.

"Fill these out and sign them. Have your parents co-sign them if you're under the age of eighteen. Make sure you understand the liability waiver." He handed Fil one of the waivers and gave Joe the other one.

"We do contracts here" Explained Mr. Cain. "One year is the most expensive. The longer you agree to the less expensive it is." He passed them to Joe and Fil.

"You can start tomorrow. You need a good mouthpiece and a groin protector. You will buy the rest of you equipment from me and it will be ordered by the end of your first month. Any questions?" He leaned back in his chair and waited.

Fil and Joe looked at each other. He could tell Joe was eager to sign up, but he had questions he wanted to ask and other schools to investigate.

"Yes Sir." Said Fil. "How much is it a month?" Cain frowned. "Didn't you hear me say you signed up by the year? One year is seven hundred twenty dollars, two years is thirteen hundred and twenty dollars and three years, our best deal, is eighteen hundred dollars. You pay thirty five dollars extra for every test up to black belt and and hundred dollars testing fee for first Dan."

Cain leaned back in his chair, the squeaks very audible in the enclosed space. "Any other questions?"

Fil had noted the arrogance that seeped into the Karate Master's voice and it made him uneasy. He wanted to find out about the workouts and Cain's philosophy about the martial arts, but was nervous about asking. "Oh well," he thought, "in for a penny, in for a pound!"

He cleared his throat and asked "what is your viewpoint on being a Christian and taking the martial arts?'

Cain looked a Fil through dubious eyes and snorted through his nose. "I think anyone can take the arts without having to worry about their immortal soul. It doesn't matter to me if I whip a believer or nonbeliever. I don't believe in religion, boy!" I believe in myself and these." He held up a pair of fists that were hugely knuckled and had a cornucopia of healed scars.

A timid knock on the office doorjamb interrupted them. Cain looked at the nervous looking purple belt. "Yes?" He questioned.

"We're done stretching, master." The purple belt looked as if he wished he could be somewhere else. "What do you wish to be done next, Sir?"

"Kicks and defends! You should of known that!" His voice dropped an octave and in undertone, "Mr. Matthews?"

"Yes Sir?" Gulped the purple belt.

"Don't ever interrupt me again. Do you comprehend me?"

"Yes Sir!" The purple belt stiffened and bowed from the waist. "Permission to go, Sir!"

Affable now, Cain granted the purple belt permission to leave and watched as he fled quickly from the office. "Gotta have discipline. That's part of the arts. No discipline, no respect and you lose what the arts are all about." He looked at Joe and Fil's hooded eyes. "You'll get used to it."

Fil could hear the purple belt, Matthews start the kicking exercise, He would have liked to watch them start out, but Mr. Cain wasn't finished with them yet.

"You have the opportunity to work with the best. We have the best program and the best instructor around." Cain's fist hooked towards his chest, thumb thrust inward. "That's me! Never been beaten in free sparring and very seldom in katas." He leaned back in his chair, satisfied that these two young men would have the proper respect for him after his lecture.

"You can go and watch them workout, tonight is free, and tomorrow you either sign up with the best or be like all the rest!" Cain stood up and herded the boys out of the office and into the workout area.

"Grab a seat gentleman and learn what it's all about." The class finished up the kicking exercise and went into defends. Simple blocks for different techniques, such as kicks, punches and multiple attacks. Fil found them fascinating.

After endless periods of kicking, punching and combinations of both, the students were ordered to get their fighting gear on.

They put on shin and instep protectors made of foam rubber covered with cloth and put suede soled foam boots over top of the. Head gear made of some type of poly coated foam for their heads and fist and forearm protectors fashioned after the foot wear were woven for arm protection.

They all sat on the floor by the sidewall and waited.

Cain went to the two lines in the middle of floor and eyed the sitting martial artists. "Who wants me first?" He asked.

One medium sized young man held his hand up and Cain motioned him up and they faced each other from their respective starting lines. Another young man holding a stopwatch stepped up to the two fighters.

"Face here!" He commanded, bow!" They did, and then Cain and the young man turned to each other and bowed again.

"Fighting positions!" Commanded the man with the stopwatch. Joe and Fil startled slightly as both Cain and his opponent, loudly "kiaed" and jumped into a fierce pose. "Begin!" The young man stepped back away from the competitors and pressed the start button to begin timing the bout.

Fil had watched enough of Chuck Norris, Jean Claude Van Damme and Steven Segal to know what most of the kicks were, so he knew the young man had led off with a front kick. He was impressed by how quickly the man had leaped towards Cain with a flurry of attacks. One, two, three kicks were thrown and several punches..... yet not one of them touched the extremely smooth and fast moving Cain.

Even with his inexperience with the martial arts, Fil could see why Cain had a master's rank. He moved like a cat and seemed to be in excellent shape. Thirty seconds had passed with his lesser opponent continually throwing technique after technique and he never came close to touching him. Cain never blocked, but always seemed to be just out of reach. A minute and a half into the fight, Cain hadn't broken a sweat yet and was still breathing clean. His opponent was starting to slow down.

"Thirty seconds left." Said the timekeeper. Cain brushed aside another ineffectual punch and exploded into a dervish of combinations. Front kick, left handed punch, right handed punch, side kick and a spinning back kick to the side of the head drove the young man back and down to the floor. Cain drove ahead and kicked the prostrate man in the buttocks.

"Ground guard!!!!!" Screamed Cain. "I showed you that technique last class!" He kicked him again. "I don't care if you are a yellow belt, you should be able to react instantly!"

The master shook his head and backed off in disgust talking to the rest of the class. "If you hesitate against a skilled opponent, you lose!" He eyed each student balefully. "Everyone give me one hundred finger tip push ups!" He said. "Maybe next time the yellow belt will remember what to do."

"Yes Sir!" The class screamed out in unison. They all assumed the position of push ups, but crossed their legs at the ankles. When the last one finished pistoning up and down, Cain glared at the offending yellow belt. "Where is your belt?" He asked softy. The yellow belt gulped slowly and answered with a low voice, "I forgot it, Sir." Cain laughed, not a pleasant sound to Fil. "You forgot it?" Repeated Cain. "After you do a thousand push ups, go sit with the white belts." "Yes Sir!" Screamed the yellow belt. Cain stepped forward and tapped his big index finger on the young man's chest. "Don't forget it again!" Cain snarled nastily. "You do and you'll regret it." "Yes Sir!" Said the yellow belt. He backed away from his master and when he backed into the wall, he dropped down and started his interminable punishment.

Fil was extremely uncomfortable with what just happened and sneaked a look at Joe. Joe was not missing a move. He seemed engrossed with what was occurring.

Not so with Fil, not only was he embarrassed for the humiliated yellow belt but was extremely discomfited for him self. He didn't know if he wanted to work out with someone like Cain teaching. He wanted to learn self-defense, yes, but he wanted to have fun also.

Fil nudged Joe with his knee and whispered. "Ready to go?" "No let's watch the whole class." Joe murmured.

Cain instantly wheeled about. "There will be no talking unless I give you permission." He winked at Joe and Fil. "Do you understand me?" He asked. Joe imitated the rank belts and said. "Yes sir!" Fil gave a precipitous nod.

"Next!" Yelled the master. Fil watched Master Cain dismantle each of the students in order. There was no repeat of the earlier incident and Fil was glad. There was only the purple belt, Mathews left and Cain called him up. "Last fight." He said.

Mathews was a lot more skilled then what the previous fighters were. He didn't rush in, but worked his way around the master looking for an opening. Cain started to get impatient and spit his mouthpiece out. "C'mon Mathews, we don't have all day!" He put his guard back in and threw a right handed back fist towards the purple belt's head. Mathews instantly blocked with what Fil thought was called a high single knife. Leaving the blocking hand up, he stepped through Cain's guard and threaded his right hand up and around the master's neck. Jerking down quick and hard, Matthews managed to flip his master to the floor. While Cain was rolling to a stop, the purple belt attacked him with an ax kick to the top of the head. Even though he controlled it to the best of his ability, the contact produced an audible slap.

Fil heard the rest of the class ooh and ahh, and even though he couldn't prove it, a snicker. Cain's face was a juxtaposition of black clouds and lightning, a thunderstorm of rage.

He snapped a hard front kick to Matthew's groin, striking deep with his right foot. As the purple belt gargled a strained scream from his closed throat and bent forward at the waist, the enraged master launched an uppercut from below his waist. He struck the stricken Matthew's under the jaw, producing a gristly popping noise, lifting him from his feet and depositing him semi-conscious on his butt in a slumping sitting position. Matthew's sat there for a long second before he continued to fall back into a splayed out x.

Cain straightened up into a solid standing position and visibly brought himself under control. Rolling his head around in a circle and then shrugging his shoulders ahead. He glanced down at the incapacitated Matthews and then ran his gaze along the wall daring one of the students to meet his piercing gaze. When none did, he shifted his eyes to Fil and Joe. It sickened Fil to see the glint of humor in his eyes.

"Sorry you had to see this disciplinary action boys." He said with a smile. "We don't allow cheap shots to go unpunished in here."

Fil held Cain's eyes for a grief second, not understanding what he had seen there. Maybe what he thought was humor was wrong. Fil though maybe the look was one of pride.

"Line up class." Cain ordered. Everyone jumped to their feet and ran to the front of the class and queued up. Arms akimbo and hands to their belly buttons.

Fil looked over at the fallen Matthews and was surprised when he unsteadily gained his feet and took his place in line.

"Face the flags!" "Bow!" "Face here!" "Bow!" Cain faced the class and said. "Matthews, stay here. I want to discuss your attitude problem." "Yes sir!" the purple belt agreed. "Class dismissed!" Cain yelled loudly.

"Yes Sir!" was the answer back, as the class yelled in unison. They quickly gathered up their bags and stripping off their gear to put the equipment in them. It didn't take long for them to stampede their way from the dojo.

Smiling, Master Cain stepped over to the two would be students and offered them his hand. Joe took it willingly and pumped it up and down with vigor. Fil was less enthusiastic. "Well boys!" Enthused Cain. "I'll see you tomorrow!" "Yeah! Sure!" Stated Joe. "We'll be here!" "Wait a minute Joe." Fil hesitated and kept Cain in his peripheral vision. "We've someplace else to go then." "What? Where?" Asked Joe. "Where we discussed earlier." Fil was exasperated. He didn't want to mention another Karate School in front of the volatile master.

Joe didn't take the hint. "Where?" He repeated. "The other Karate School." Under toned Fil. Cain's head jerked slightly. "There's only one other school around here and that's Brown's Karate!" "You're not thinking about that dojo are you?" He demanded.

Fil faced the irked master and nodded "Yes, yes we are." Cain laughed aloud in disbelief. "Didn't you hear what

I said earlier?" He asked. "I told you that I'm the best!" Don't waste your time with a washed up has been!"

Fil was tired of all the bluster and was ready to leave. "Let's go!" He said to Joe and turned to leave. "Don't you turn your back on me!" Cain retorted. He grabbed Fil by the shoulder and jerked him around thrusting his reddened face into Fils.

"I'm offering you this one opportunity." He snarled. "You don't show up tomorrow ready to work out, don't come back at all." He released his grip and gave Fil a slight shove backwards. He fixed his gaze on Joe. "Same thing goes for you!" Cain wheeled around shouting for Matthews to meet him in the office. Shaken, Fil pulled the door open and left the building followed by Joe.

Fil drove slower then the 55 mile an hour speed limit on the way home and neither he nor Joe had anything to say. Each was lost in their thoughts. They pulled up to Joe's house and as Joe exited the vehicle, he said "see you at school." "Yeah later." Fil pulled away. Fil went to his home, kissed his parents good night and laid awake half the night before falling in an uneasy rest.

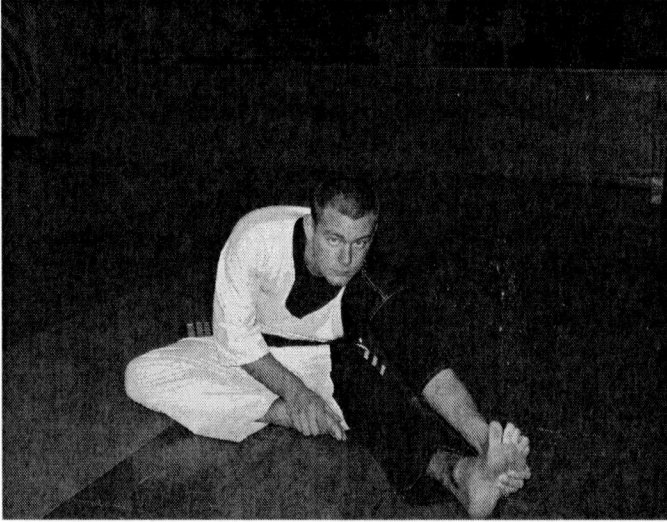

CHAPTER FOUR

The next day at school Joe caught up with Fil at lunch as usual. Shame faced, Joe told him he couldn't go with Fil to Brown's Karate that evening. Fil didn't ask why. He didn't have too. His best friend was seduced by the raw power that was emanating from the obstreperous Master Cain. Joe did his best to convince Fil to join him, but Fil politely declined. If the visit didn't pan out tonight then Fil would rather give up his fledgling hope of being a martial artist rather than be associated with the capricious Cain.

He found a secluded nook and prayed silently to his Lord. He needed the refuge of God. After his prayer he felt more at ease.

After school he went to work and then home. He showered and tried to take a brief nap, although his nerves were too jangled to allow him to drop off. Six thirty came and he was off to seek his future.

CHAPTER FIVE

Fil had a bit of trouble locating the dojo. Not that it was secluded, but it was a little ways from town.

His father had told him how to find the place and as usual his directions were right on. Fil had missed the school on the way down the pastoral road but found it after he had turned around and came back.

It was a nondescript block building with a small sign adorning the façade. Squinting, he found the sign spelled out "Brown Karate."

This was it then. He sat in the car for a long minute, musing. He decided that if Brown were anything like

Cain, he would leave. He didn't want a repeat of last night. Tomorrow was the last day of school; maybe he could pick up another part time job to fill his summer hours.

He exited the car and approached the building. He thought he heard something and paused. He heard it again and realized it was the tickled laugh of a young child. Fil thought the mirth incongruous after the severe atmosphere of Cain's dojo the previous evening.

Hesitantly, he opened the door of the dojo and entered. Directly in front of him was a trophy case. The most prominent feature was a picture of a man in a blue uniform or gi, as the martial artists call the outfit they wear. Fil was proud of himself. After seeing Cain's students so sensational in their glamorous uniforms, he had looked up the name of them and had come up with "gi".

The man in the picture had an array of medals hanging from his neck and most of them were gold. In his hand was a long staff.

Fil looked the rest of the trophies over and realized that different students had won them. Their names were taped to the marble bases.

Laughter floated lightly from an open door leading into a room that Fil couldn't see into. He eased himself over and peered inside. There in the middle of the carpeted floor, were three people composing a triangle playing with a hacky-sack. They were very adroit with their feet as they passed the sack back and forth. The adult missed it prompting another spate of laughter from the two young boys. One of the youths saw Fil and said, "Mr. Brown," and pointed at him. "OH! Hello." Said the man. He picked up the hacky-sack and flipped it to one of the boys. "Keep practicing."

He walked over to Fil and offered his hand. "Major Brown." "Can I help you?" He asked as he gave Fil's hand a firm grip and a short pump.

He was about the same size as Fil, but harder. Mr. Brown was muscular without looking buff. His sandy brown hair was tinged with gray, but his face was youthful and unlined. He moved as if he had a sore back, but still seemed lithe. Fil liked the looks of him already. " I'm interested in classes."

Brown looked him up and down missing no detail. "C'mon out and take a seat." Was all he said. Fil followed him out expecting to go to the office and was surprised when they sat on the couch that was in the small lobby.

Brown reached over and grabbed a sweat top that was lying on the chair that matched the couch and slipped it on. The green outfit matched the instructor's eyes.

"What's your name?" "Fil Hooper, sir." He answered." "Hooper. Huh?" He asked, "any relation to Carl?" Surprised that he knew his father, Fil nodded. He would ask his dad about it later. Brown stared into Fil's eyes and to the young man's credit; he didn't try to avoid the instructor's gaze.

"Why do you want to be a martial artist?" He asked.

Fil thought for a moment before he replied. He didn't want to give an ambiguous answer. "I want the ability to defend myself." He said. "I want the option to be able to fight or to shun a fight."

Brown leaned back on the couch. "Are you the one who fought Link Smith yesterday?" He queried.

Dumb founded, Fil again just nodded. "Is that why you're here?" He asked.

Fil found his voice, amazed that the martial artist knew what was going on at his school. "Well Mr. Brown, I' didn't really fight him. I didn't throw a punch. I'm here because I hope to circumvent any more of these types of incidents."

Satisfied Major leaned forward. "Here's what you need to know." He cleared this throat and begun the same discourse that he had given to many other neophyte martial artists. "Classes are twice a week with an occasional Saturday. Tuesday and Wednesday from 7:00 to 8:30. You don't need a Gi right away, but eventually you'll need one if you want to stick with it. I have sparring equipment you can borrow, but again you'll want your own if you stay.

"I don't recommend buying a lot of equipment because of the cost. Once you decide you are truly going to stay the course, by all means, order the equipment." He explained. "You're on a months probation. I won't discharge a long time student if the two of you can't get along. Loyalty is an important facet of the arts and I'm dedicated to my people."

"Okay Mr. Brown." Agreed Fil.

"I'll let you know when you're ready to test or capable of fighting tournaments. Defense is the key there. I don't want anyone hurt. We practice controlled sparring. I go on the premise that we have to go to work tomorrow and we don't go to work injured." Major Brown thought for a moment. "All black belts are Miss, Mrs. or Mr. I don't care what age they are. They earned their respect. Bow on your way into the workout and bow on your way out. When you are in there, you are in martial arts country and you show respect. We also bow to each other for the same reason. I think that's about it." He said. "Any questions?"

Fil didn't want to upset Mr. Brown, but he had to ask him the same question he had asked Dean A. Cain. "Do you have any problems with a Christian working out with your class?" He asked. "Not at all." Said Major. "I'm a Christian too." Relieved, Fil asked. "What are your view point of Christianity and the Eastern Arts?"

"I don't teach the dark side of the arts." Said Brown. "Chi power and the esoteric parts if the arts go against my beliefs."

"I know this will sound stupid, but can I ask you one more question?" Fil asked.

"There is no stupid queries if you're sincere. Ask away."

Shyly Fil asked. "What do you think God thinks about the martial arts? Because of the martial arts being a fighting sport?"

Major laughed. "Do you read the Bible?' "Yes Sir." Replied Fil.

"Do you know why God changed Jacob's name to Israel?" He asked. "Do you know what Israel means?"

Fil searched his memory. Chagrined, he had to admit he didn't know. "No sir, I don't."

"Israel is Jewish for God strives or He who strives with God. Jacob received the name when he wrestled the night away with our God. I figure that if God likes wrestling, then he likes other sports. Look it up in Genesis 32: verses 22-31 and see what you think." Smiled Major.

More students came through the door-greeting Major by lightly banging knuckles together. The classroom was rapidly filling up.

"Tell you what, Fil. You are more then welcome to watch tonight. The next class is free, then it's $35 a month after that."

"Wow! That's cheaper then Cain's classes are!" He exclaimed. Chagrined, he realized what he had espoused. "Here we go." He thought, a lecture about being the best school around. He was surprised when Major grinned and said, "none cheaper, c'mon in. It's time to start."

It was a nice size class, twelve of them not counting Major Brown. Fil recognized one of the older students. He was in one of Fil's classes, but he was a freshman. This was probably Brown's source of information from the high school.

"Line up please." Major turned and faced the flags, "bow," he turned and faced the two lines of students. "Face here, bow!"

"Everyone! Attention please!" Brown pointed to Fil. "This is Fil Hooper. He's thinking about lessons. Fil nodded his head to each person as Mr. Brown named them. It was a lot friendlier atmosphere then the previous evening. Fil found himself relaxing. Mr. Brown called the top ranked student up to run the stretching.

Fil couldn't tell what rank anyone was because no one wore belts. Several had on gi pants but there wasn't anyone in the formal uniform so prevalent in Cain's school last night.

As the exercises commenced, Brown walked around the students and straightened a leg here, corrected several other little forms that the students weren't doing precisely, all the time giving encouragement and praise.

The lead student continued the exercises as Mr. Brown came over to the bench and sat down beside Fil. They both watched the martial artists exert themselves for a few moments, before Brown began to softly speak.

"We're here to have a good time. I maintain discipline, but I'm not as strict as most Karate dojos are!" Brown raised his voice. "Put you minds in your muscles!!! Get loose!!!"

The students redoubled their efforts. Satisfied, Brown began to speak again.

"There's a time to be serious, and a time for fun. I demand respect, but I also want your friendship. As long as I'm having fun, I'll be teaching. As soon as it's work, I'm done."

He glanced at Fil. "Understand?" He asked. "Yes Sir." Fil said, amazed how easily he had come to respect this man already. 'Wear what you want in here to workout, but I don't allow anything offensive and that includes alcohol and cigarette ads on your tee shirts."

The lead student faced Mr. Brown and bowed with respect. "We're ready, Sir!" Brown returned the bow and thanked him. "Line up! Two lines!" He yelled. The students jumped in line.

Mr. Brown ran them quickly through the same defends that was practiced last night at the Cain Dojo. He ran them through quickly and then preceded into kicking exercises. The students worked diligently on their form and kiaed loudly.

The master ran them through the kicks fairly rapidly and then went to a punching exercise called kemo-say.

They assumed a stance that hunkered them down into a stance that made them look as if they were astride a horse and threw a series of punches on Mr. Brown's commands.

Sweat was rolling off all of the students when Brown finally called a halt to the fast paced work out.

"Face here!" He shouted. "Bow." Everyone bowed. "Get a drink and get you fighting gear on."

As the students moved to obey, Fil was amazed when a couple of the students came over and sat down on either side of him.

"I'm Daniel." Said one. "I'm Jase." Said the other one.

Fil shook hands with both of them warmed by the friendly attitude extended by both. "This looks like a good place to work out." He said.

"None better." Said Daniel. "I've been here four years and have enjoyed it all."

Jase agreed. "I've been here two years, but it seems like a second home to me."

Daniel looked at Fil with curiousity. "I've seen you in school. You hang around with Joe Ryan, don't you?" He asked. "Yes I do. He's my best friend." Replied Fil.

"Is he thinking about signing up too?" Queried Jase.

Fil simply shook his head. "That's a shame." Said Daniel. "We could use some more size in here."

Mr. Brown came back into the workout area carrying a stopwatch. "Who's ready?" He asked.

Daniel and Jase stood up and went to the center of the floor. They pulled their headgears on and put their mouthpieces in.

They faced Mr. Brown and bowed, then each other and bowed again. They reached out and touched knuckles together. Mr. Brown looked over at Fil. "That means that we're friends." He explained. "If excessive contact is made, then we know it's accidental."

"Begin!" Commanded Mr. Brown.

The combatants circled each other warily, each looking for the opportunity to strike. Daniel throw first. He feinted a kick low to the knee and instantly threw a second kick to Jases's head. Fooled badly, Jase reached to defend the initial kick only to be struck by a controlled round house to the side of his headgear.

"Point!" Shouted Mr. Brown. "Acknowledge!" The two fighters reached out and lightly tapped knuckles, then resumed fighting positions.

"Begin!"

They started to circle each other again and this time Jase led off with a flurry of techniques.

A side kick to the stomach; followed by a spin kick, a spinning crescent and another sidekick aimed for the midsection were all blocked adroitly by Daniel.

Again they circled. Daniel led off with a quick back fist trying to catch Jase off guard. It didn't and Jase blocked it down following the block with a scoring reverse punch to the mid section.

"Point!" Shouted Mr. Brown. "And time."

"Face here!" The fighters went to their respective starting lines and faced the master. "Bow!" The complied. "Face each other! Bow! Have a seat!" Browned eyed the sitting fighters. "Who's next?" He asked.

Fill watched astounded. The free sparring he was watching differed immensely from the debacle he witnessed last night. He admired the expertise each artist commanded. He wasn't sure, but he thought that such a deft touch had to be harder skill to conquer then the uncontrolled aggression of the hostile Master Cain.

"Daniel, take the watch." Said Mr. Brown. "Yes Sir!" Said Daniel as he moved smoothly and confidently to take over the head juror's duties.

Major Brown's eschewed the headgear, but fitted a boxer's mouthpiece in. He pointed to the first fighter in line and sparred for 60 seconds and then moved to the next one. He sparred each of them and offered encouragement and praise as some aspect of each fighter appealed to him.

Fil kept waiting for Major Brown to gain the upper hand and to establish his superiority over each fighter, but he never did. In fact, it looked as if Mr. Brown tailored his fighting skills to match that of his competitor.

"Nah!" Thought Fil. "Why would he do that?"

Too soon, Mr. Brown was lining them up to dismiss them for the evening.

After bowing out, the artists gathered up their equipment and prepared to leave. All of them either said goodbye or nodded to him as they left. Fil felt like he was wanted here.

Mr. Brown stood by the exit and had a comment for each of the students as they left. Everyone left with a smile on his face, even the parents that had arrived early to watch the end of class.

"This is terrific." Thought Fil.

Soon, Fil and Mr. Brown were the only ones left. "Come into the office." Major walked into the small cubicle and sat down at his desk. He motioned Fil to battered seat.

"Well, what do you think?" He asked Fil.

"I like it."

"Great! I think you would fit in with everyone here. When do you want to start?"

Fil would of loved to say tomorrow, but he had promised his father he would discuss it with him first. Fil always tried to keep his word. Especially when dealing with his dad.

"I have to talk it over with my father first." Said Fil. "I could let you know later this evening if you like." Fil noticed Major was looking through him, his thoughts somewhere else.

"Sir?" He questioned.

"Eh? OH… Yes that's fine." Major leaned back in the chair and steeple his fingers by his lips. "Tell your father I said hello."

He handed Fil the necessary paper work and stood up offering his hand to the teen.

"You don't need to call me. If your father allows you, be here tomorrow."

"Yes Sir! Thank you." Fil shook the master's hand and took his leave.

CHAPTER SIX

Fil was excited. The ride home seemed to last only a second. He pounded up the

steps to the house and banged his way noisily in. "Dad!" He yelled. Carl Hooper emerged from the kitchen, noshing on a skinned carrot.

"Hey Son, how'd it go?" He said through a mouthful of carrot.

"Great Dad. Mr. Brown said to say hello. How do you know him? He seemed nice!"

"Slow down, Fil." Laughed Mr. Hooper. "You seem very excited."

"I am. It was so much different then last night. You should have seen them, Dad."

Fil followed his father into the living room. Carl sat down and listened to his excited boy tell about all he had seen and heard at the dojo.

When he finally concluded his tale. Fil went back to his original question. "He seemed cool, Dad, but he acted like you were friends. Do you know him very well?"

In answer, Carl Hooper reached down beside his chair and pulled an old duffle bag into view. He tossed it to Fil, who caught it easily.

"Open it up." Said Carl.

Fil pulled on the over sized zipper and listened to the hard rasp as he unzipped it. Peering inside, he was astounded. It was equipment, martial arts gear. He reached in and pulled out a glove similar to the ones he'd seen in the last two evenings. The glove and the boots that followed were beat up and duct taped in a piecemeal fashion, but were still very serviceable. Digging further, he found a gi. It was black and faded but still in good shape. A 3x5 U.S.A. flag was on the left shoulder and a Korean flag of the same size adorned the right. A Brown's Karate patch was centered over the left breast area. On the very bottom of the duffle was a black belt with one white stripe and several red ones adorning it.

Puzzled, Fil asked. "Whose gear is this, Dad?"

Chuckling, Carl answer was brief. "Mine."

Fil's eyes met his fathers. "Yours? Wow Dad, you're a black belt?"

"Yes I am. I hold a black belt in Tae Kwon Do and one in quarter staff fighting." He paused, waiting.

"Geez, why didn't you tell me? I think this is great." Said Fil.

"It was a while ago. I quit being active after you were born." Replied Carl. "A good black belt doesn't have to let everyone know what he is. He should be satisfied with his skills and knowledge."

Fil nodded his acknowledgement as his father continued.

"We're about the same size and you can use my equipment, all but the belt."

"They weren't wearing belts tonight, is there a reason for that?"

Carl's brow creased as he replied, "Major Brown is laid back, but he was probably holding an informal class tonight. Wear the gi and I know where my old white belt is. You need it."

"Great Dad, I appreciate it. Tell me about you career."

Carl pursed his lips and steeple his fingers as he thought back.

"I worked out in the arts for several years." He said. "Near the end I taught Major's classes." Carl paused, clearly uneasy. "I don't know how much to tell you. I don't like to spread falsehoods or innuendos about anyone, but Major Brown's child was kidnapped and he used his skills to get him back. I ran his school until he finally cleared himself with the law." He held his son's eyes with his own.

If you want to know the story, you can look it up on the internet." Leaning back in his chair, he continued. "Whatever you read, remember, there is two sides to every story. If you want to work out at his dojo, I couldn't recommend a better instructor… or man."

Fil knew his father would never give such glowing praise unless the person deserved it. That settled it. Brown's Karate it is.

"Once you start free sparring, we can practice together." Carl Hooper smiled. "That's the part I really missed. Throwing hands. Wow! I'm starting to get excited too. This is great!"

Carl flipped the television on, thought about it for a second and shut it off again.

"Do you want me to show you some stretches?"

"Boy Dad! That would be awesome."

"I'm doing it for me too." Laughed Carl. "I don't want to pop a groin muscle or pull a hammy."

Carl stood and put his arm on his son's shoulder. "C'mon, let's go to the basement and get started." They went down the steps, Fil in the lead and both had big smiles animating their faces.

CHAPTER SEVEN

Fil awoke the next morning with a smile on his face. The sun was up and he could hear the birds chirping from outside his window.

Lying on his back, he closed his eyes and prayed.

"Dear Lord, Thank you for the restful night. Thank you for this day and for my family and friends. Help me make it through this day by being a strong witness for you. Amen."

His morning prayer done, Fil sat up and swung his legs over the side of his bed and started to rise.

"Holy Cow!" He thought. "I'm sore!"

He thought back to last night and the stretches his father put him through. He could feel his muscles and tendons pulling, but his father had been adamant about how far he could bend.

"It'll take you awhile to get truly flexible." He said. "This is an important facet of the arts that often doesn't receive the respect it deserves. Work hard at it every day and you'll be surprised at what you can achieve."

What had greatly surprised Fil was how supple and flexible Carl Hooper was. As he showed Fil the proper techniques for a perfect position, he had no problem doing them. He had to admit he was impressed.

Fil had never thought about his father being athletic. He was… well, just dad.

They had stretched for a half an hour before Carl Hooper had called halt.

"That is what you'll do tomorrow. Before you head to the dojo, you might want to loosen up. Do what we did tonight, but remember, stretch till it is a little uncomfortable, not till it hurts.

Fil got up from the bed and reached towards the ceiling as he alternately tightened and loosened the muscles of his body. "Boy! That felt good!"

He dropped to the floor and assumed the first position his dad showed him. He sat on his butt with his legs in a "vee" position before him, toes pointing up. He slowly bent forward at the waist and tried to put his forehead to the floor without letting his knees come up from the floor. He worked on it until, finally his forehead touched the floor and he held it for a seven count. Moving to the next stretch, he simply pulled his right foot back to his crotch area. One leg still extended.

He worked down over top of his knee, then to the inside and outside. He finished up on a 45-degree angle and then switched legs. He went through the same motions and slowly worked the stiffness from his muscles. He put both legs out in front of him and grabbed the tips of his toes. He kept his knees straight and pulled back.

He let go and assumed a hurdler stretch on the floor. Again he worked over the top and both sides of the knee. He leaned back and lay on the floor. He carefully bounced the bent knee and after every seven count, he changed from bouncing to clamping the tip of the to the floor.

He sat back up and switched to the other side and stretched that side too. He stood up and took a wide stance. He bent at the waist, again keeping his knees locked. He slowly walked hand over hand back and forth to each foot and "twinge" each hamstring.

Finally loose, he stood and shook the muscles in his arms.

"Man! I feel good!" He thought, as he went to the bathroom to begin his day.

CHAPTER EIGHT

Last day of school, truly not a workday, but a leisure day. Even the most straight-laced teachers are relaxed. A lot of the teen wouldn't see each other until the next school year.

That was okay with Fil. He was planning on working more at his job at the retail store and picking up extra money. He couldn't let his mother and father pay for his katate lessons.

Money was always a concern. His car ate up quite a few bucks. Gas was high and even though he didn't have a steady girl friend, he still liked to socialize every now and then. Add $35.00 to his budget and he would be strained for a while. Thank goodness his father had the karate gear. That would of really put a bite on him.

Oh well, he wasn't going to worry about it. He always seemed to get by. He always thanked God for that. Every since he accepted Christ as his Lord and Savior, he seemed to always make it. Inwardly, in his thoughts, he again thanked God. How great it is to be living in the blessing of the Lord. He truly felt troubled that not all of his friends were Christians. In fact some of them quit coming around because he accepted Christ. He knew they were uncomfortable and tried to allay their discomfort, but still they eased away.

Jesus said it wouldn't be easy to follow him, but if this is the worst trial he ever faced, he would consider himself lucky.

He drove by Joe's house and started to park, when Joe came to the front door and waved him on.

Fil continued to school. Occasionally Joe's mother had something for him to do in the mornings, so Fil didn't consider it unusual.

He parked his car and whistled his way up the steps, smiling and nodding at everyone.

Some of the more "elite" group barely acknowledged him, yet he didn't let it perturb him. His dad always said that the so- called elite clique are rarely important in the real world. They are the ones who were taught they were better then most, but found out they weren't when they finally had to earn their way.

He went to his locker and spun the combination lock open. The inside was bare. He had turned all of his text books in the last couple of days.

Shutting his door, he leaned against it and watched his fellow students go about their morning activities. Again, he nodded or spoke to everyone who caught his eye.

Kristy, who had the locker to the right of his, stopped and dug through her locker.

" What are you planning for the summer?"

Fil had already decided to take his father's words of wisdom to heart and elected not to mention martial arts to anyone.

"Finding something to do and of course work." he answered.

"Good for you. Maybe I'll see you around?"

She raised her left eyebrow in a question mark.

Fil liked Kristy and they had casually dated through Junior High and an occasional Saturday night movie/ bowling date.

"Sure I'll call you."

She smiled and left to go to home- room. Fil smiled too. She was a cute girl and both of his parents approved of her.

He glanced at his watch and started to his home- room when he caught Joe coming in from the corner of his eye.

He turned to greet him. His hello turned to a gasp of shock when seen the lump under Joe's left eye. Not only was it knotted, a plum purple and inky black bruise covered the area around his slit eye.

"Whoa Joe!" He exclaimed. "Did you run into the wall?"

Not looking at Fil, he answered with a soft "no."

"Seriously, what happened?" Fil was concerned.

Exasperated, Joe turned. "Nothing. I…I just fell."

"You fell?" Fil was incredulous. "How did you get that falling?"

Angry now, Joe growled at Fi.l. "I said I fell! Are you calling me a liar?"

Fil was taken aback. Joe and he were friends for years and they never talked to each other in such a manner.

"No Joe, but that is nasty…" His voice trailed off as a thought occurred to him.

"You didn't fall." He accused. "You got that last night at Cain's dojo, didn't you?"

Joe looked ashamed. He blinked his eyes rapidly, trying to think of a plausible excuse.

"So…I lied." He said. "I didn't want you to hassle me about it."

"What happened? Did Cain do that to you? Cripes Joe, you can't go back there. Come with me! I start at Brown's Karate tonight. You will like him. He's great!" Said Fil.

"No, I going to learn at Cain's."

"C'mon Joe, we always do everything together. Let' do this too!"

"My parents and I signed a contract last night."

Joe paused thinking about the previous evening. "We paid for a 3 year contract.

"Oh Joe…." Started Fil.

"Stop it now!" Interrupted his friend. "I told you! I'm not going to be a door mat any longer!"

Fil felt a presence behind him and started to turn, is nose already identifying who it was.

"Nice eye, Ryan." Laughed stink. "I wish I was the one who gave it to you."

"You didn't, so leave me alone Smith." Joe was angry and unthinking.

Instantly stinks right hand flashed up and with a hard open hand slap, he landed it on Joe's injured eye.

He staggered back from the impact and brought his left hand up to cover his eye.

Big Stink Smith moved forward to land another.

Fil Moved smoothly in front of him. "That's enough, Link"

"Didn't you learn anything from the other day?" Asked an incredulous Smith.

"It's the last day, Link! Give us a break."

Link hesitated, head down, he glowered at both boys. Then t o Fil's astonishment, he turned and left.

"You okay Joe?"

"He's going to pay! Anyone who has ever crossed me is going to pay!" Joe was so angry he was spitting his words. "You wait and see!" Joe turned and ran from the school building.

Fil debated about following him and decided to let his friend work it out on his own.

If someone would had told him that he and Joe would not be hanging out together that summer, he would of scoffed and dismissed such nonsense.

He shrugged his shoulders and headed to homeroom.

CHAPTER NINE

Fil was sweating heavily and breathing harder. "Breath in through the nose and out through the mouth!" Commanded Master Brown. "In order to fight continuously, you must control your breathing."

Fil was two weeks into karate. It had been obvious to Major Brown that his newest pupil had a major talent and could be one of the best students he ever had. He listened to every word and nuance of Major's teaching and absorbed it all as if his entire life depended on getting everything down to perfection.

He had him working on the heavy bag at the moment. Fil was going full power using both hands and legs. Throwing punches, elbows and palm heel techniques and then quickly switching to side- kicks, round-house, front and an occasional spin kick, he was fast approaching exhaustion.

Major had a stopwatch on him and he was 30 seconds short of 5 minutes.

"Harder …Faster…Control your breathing!" Extolled Major.

He held the stopwatch at eye level and yelled. "Time!" as he pushed the stem of the stopwatch down. "One minute breather." Said Major. "Assume your position."

Fil dropped to his knees, feet behind him, toes down, hands resting on his thighs.

He closed his eyes and ignored his body's desperate call for air as he slowly filled his lungs to capacity inhaling through his nose. Once full, he pursed his lips and gently emptied his lungs. He imagined he was drawing a long silver string smoothly in through his nose. And blowing gently out his mouth keeping the string straight and unrippled.

The first 30 seconds were torture. It took all of his strength to keep the discipline necessary to perform this exercise. His body instinctively wanted to draw in great draughts through his mouth. It would have been counter- productive.

When Fil first started doing this, Major let him do as his body dictated. The next time he had prepared him to do it correctly. He had problems at first, until he realized that it actually worked. After that it was just a matter of discipline.

Fil was also learning to breathe the same way as he free sparred. It was incredible the difference it made.

"Maki-wari board." Said Major.

Breathing freely again, Fil assumed a kemo say position in front of the canvas padded oak board.

The makiwari board was set in a steel holder that allowed it to have some spring. Fil likened it to working out on a speed bag, although the hardness and the necessity of hitting everything correctly to avoid a broken knuckle made this exercise more dangerous then the speed-bag.

"Five minutes and you're done on conditioning." Intoned Master Brown.

Fil had learned to let his mind go else where as his body worked out. It was like working outing in front of a television set. If the program was good, you didn't know you were exerting yourself until a commercial came on. Then you became aware of muscle tightness and labored breathing. It was the same principle, but Fil let his mind go to a place of peace. He tried to keep an image of a mountain meadow in his mind. Always adding woodland creatures or perhaps the jumping of fish in a fast moving frigid stream.

"Time!'

Fil smiled as his mind came back to his body. He was amazed at his progress in the last couple of weeks. Master Brown had told him he already had the technique down. Just think how much he could accomplish after a year!

He felt good! His body was shedding all excess fat and he was actually starting to show a six-pack.

He sat down and started to pull on his dads borrowed gear as Major went to each of the students stations and halted the various exercises.

Everyone started to prepare for the best part of the class…free sparring.

Fil was good. Real good.

In his first class, he had fought several times with each of the bigger ranked students and a couple of times with Master Brown.

Everything was done slowly and with control. Each fighter showing an opening and explaining what move he should make to exploit the opening.

He ate it up. He picked it up quickly and by the 3rd class, they were moving close to full speed.

What really helped him was his dad.

Fil still had trouble believing his dad could move like he does.

Fil couldn't touch him. He realized that it was a lack of experience, but his father was like an ethereal cloud.

He had been impressed when he had watched Dean A. Cain move, but was totally awed by Carl Hooper. He was always one inch away. With all the sparring and instruction from the students, Master Brown and his father, Fil made a giant leap forward.

His innate intelligence and his unsuspected athleticism combined together to produce a beginning martial artist that was far ahead of the average person. Instead of being satisfied, Fil pushed harder. When he wasn't working, he was working out. It showed.

Master Brown called him and Jase up. Even though Jase had 2 years experience on him, you could of never picked that fact up by watching them free spar. Fil pushed the action by firing combination after combination. Side kicks, roundhouses, mixed with punches and crescent kicks kept Jase on the defensive. Thirty seconds into the fight Fil started to score. They didn't stop to acknowledge. Major called the points as they happened. "Beautiful fight, men." Said Master Brown when he stopped it. "Both of you. Nice defense, Jase."

Both students bowed to their master and took a seat on the floor.

Jase whispered to the artist beside him, while Fil intently watched the two who were sparring. He found he could pick up tendencies of each fighter if he watched closely enough. Each move was cataloged and added to his list to try out. If it worked out, he would use it, if not it would be discarded.

His father said he didn't have to have a lot of fancy moves, just be good with the ones he had.

He fought several more times and class was being dismissed.

They bowed before the flags, both the American and Korean, then to Master Brown. They would have bowed to any black belts too, but there was none in attendance.

"Tae Kwon Do!" They shouted to end the class.

"Fil, could I see you after class, please?" Asked Major.

"Yes Sir!" Agreed Fil.

They waited for everyone to leave and when the last one had knocked knuckles with the Master, he turned to Fil.

"You are good." He said. "I've watched you and being here such a short time, I am amazed at your progress." He smiled. "I figure that dad has been working with you I can see it in your sparring."

"Yes Sir. He has."

"At the end of summer a friend of mine always holds a tournament. How would you like to fight in it?"

"Me? Do you think I'll be ready?"

"I wouldn't asked you if I didn't think so." He said. "I need some help in the dojo. Would you be willing to clean up and do whatever is needed in exchange for private lessons?"

"Absolutely Sir!" Fil was excited. "I can still come to regular class too, can't I?"

"Sure can. You can only make the other students better. I'll tell you what. Tell your dad he is welcome to work out with us."

"Really Sir?"

"Really."

Fil reached over and clasped hands with the Master. "I'll ask him. Thank you, Sir!"

"Your welcome. First lesson tomorrow at 10:00."

Fil grinned. "I'll be there."

On his way home, Fil again thanked God for blessing him.

His dad, to his surprise, agreed to work out with him and Major Brown.

What a summer this was going to be.

CHAPTER TEN

Fil worked hard all summer, learning to throw a bladed side- kick to perfection. His timing was impeccable and he finally was able to score upon both his father and Master Brown

He progressed so rapidly that he was awarded his yellow belt, jumped to ninth orange, tested again and was currently an eight blue.

Both his father and Master Brown said he was fighting near black belt level. Experience would place him closer to that plateau.

School was starting a week from Monday and this weekend was his first tournament. Butterflies were already prevalent in his stomach and he had two days to wait.

CHAPTER ELEVEN

Saturday came quickly and he and his father met Master Brown at the tournament site.

Everyone they talked to knew both Major Brown and Carl Hooper. To Fil, It appeared that both gentlemen were once fierce and mighty competitors in their division. Everyone was pleased to meet Fil and wished him luck at his first tourney.

As the trio made the circuit around the gym, Major introduced Fil to the promoter. He was a black man, well featured, and powerfully built. He wore a purple-based outfit and was very flamboyant. Years later he would die in a fire trying to rescue someone who wasn't home.

Fil found a quiet corner and started to stretch out. It was one of his favorite parts of the arts. It gave him time to himself and he prayed as he stretched. "Lord, I'm not asking you to help me win today. All I'm asking you is give me the opportunity to do my best. Let me honor you in both actions and deeds. Thank you for this time to be with two good Christian men and being in fellowship with my fellow martial artists." He opened his eyes. "Amen!"

He looked across the crowd and was both shocked and pleased. Standing beside Master Dean A. Cain was his friend Joe.

He rose to his feet and headed to his friend. It took him some time to get there, as much as he wanted to get to Joe, He still obeyed the protocol dictated to him by both his father and Master Brown

He paid respect to each black belt he encountered by bowing and said hello to any gup rank that caught his eye.

Finally, with a huge grin, he stood in front of Joe.

"It's great to see you, Joe!" He exclaimed. "I haven't seen you all summer. This great! Are you fighting today too? Wow! Maybe we'll be in the same division!"

Fil was happy to be able to talk to Joe. He had called his house numerous times and had dropped by several times, but like Fil, Joe always seemed to be at Karate class.

Something was wrong. Joe looked uneasy and looked around the gym, not wanting to meet Fil's eyes.

"What's the matter Joe? Aren't you glad to see me?" He asked.

Master Cain slipped forward and thrust an arm between Joe and Fil.

"He came to fight, not make friends."

Fil was taken aback."

"What do you mean, make friends? Joe and I have been pals forever."

"Not any more, you are in the same division. You are the enemy." Cain moved forward aggressively moving between Joe and Fil. "Beat it, kid!"

Fil looked around Cain's bulk, trying to catch Joe's eye. "Is this for real, Joe? C'mon it's your buddy, Fil."

Finally, Joe looked at Fil. "I don't have any buddies." He turned and walked away. Cain smirked and took two steps backwards before turning and catching up with Joe.

Fil stood still, his face flaming with embarrassment. His old buddy Joe had blown him off. He couldn't believe it.

He watched as many of the same people who had wholly embraced his father, Master Brown and himself, turn away from Master Cain and Joe as if they had encountered a putrid odor.

"Dad! Did you see what just happened?"

"I saw, son. Joe is mixed up with a rotten apple and some of the slime is rubbing off on him."

Fil was shocked at what his father had just said. That was the strongest condemnation he ever heard his father issue. Cain must be worse then he thought.

"Forget about it son. You need to start thinking about the tournament."

CHAPTER TWELVE

Fil's bracket had started and there were

a total of fourteen fighters in his division. Sure enough Joe and he was in together. If they and kept winning, they would eventually meet.

Fil had fought first and had beaten his opponent fairly easily. Final score five to one.

There was a match before Joe's and as was his usual habit, Fil filed away each fighters tendencies.

Not all of the fighters were good. It was a mixed group, beginners to less then a year artists. Not a good mix for neophyte fighters.

Joe came out and faced a beginner. It was over almost before it started. With unbelievable speed, Joe threw a sidekick straight to the gut of the white belt, following it with a back fist to the side of the head. The white belt dropped to the floor. After several minutes he rose, but forfeited his match to Joe.

Fil heard grumbling from the crowd about dirty fighting and "unnecessary roughness." Fil could tell it didn't bother either Cain or Joe.

Fil won his second fight again five to one. He touched knuckles with his opponent and told him "nice job." The fighter smiled and thanked him.

Again it was Joe's turn. Fil couldn't imagine that Joe was as good as he was. He never was good at anything except for schoolwork. Joe moved like a young Cain. Suppressed power in each move. His arms were muscular and veined. Boy, he sure looked different.

He threw a front kick hard to the blue belt's stomach, which was blocked. He instantly spun into a spinning back fist. He caught him on the helmet by the temple using a full force blow. He dropped him. It was a legal blow, but Joe was warned of excessive contact. The blue belt stayed in the fight, but his spirit was gone. Joe won again easily.

Both Joe and Fil kept winning. They were clearly the best fighters and knew they would meet in the final.

The difference between the fighters was attitude.

Fil was enjoying his first tournament and his fights. He had a compliment for each fighter he disposed.

Joe on the other hand, didn't acknowledge his opponents at all. He barely showed respect by bowing. Basically, his bow consisted of barely bending at the waist and a slight nod of the head.

Two fighters squared off to decide who would take home the third place trophy. The loser received a ribbon. It was an exciting bout and it stimulated the crowd. The artist who won it was one of Fil's previous matches. He ground it out five to four and he bumped hands with Fil when he came off of the floor.

Finally.........

It was time for the two fighters to go for the top prize. Fil wanted to win, but was excited to make it this far. He never expected to be in this position. Everyone told him he had the skill and talent to win this tournament, but was humble enough to realize that on any given day anyone could be beat.

The promoter called for attention and introduced the two fighters.

Fil felt proud when he called his name and his master's school.

When the promoter called Joe's name and Cain's Karate, there was a smattering of boos discernable through out the crowd.

The center referee called the two to center.

"Let's keep it clean!" He said. "This is the championship fight. Put on a good show for the people."

He stepped back. "Face here!" He commanded. "Bow!" He had both arms upraised, palms facing inward. "Face each other...Bow!" He stepped back and put his left hand between Joe and Fil.

Fil knew when his hand went up the fight would start.

"Begin!" He yelled and his hand was withdrawn.

Fil was on his toes ready to defend Joe's first attack but Joe didn't move. To Fils amazement, he held his fist out.

Fil had seen a few of the martial artists do that before. It meant they respected each other and they hoped for a good fight.

Maybe there was some decency in his old buddy Joe after all, he thought. Smiling, he relaxed and reached out with his fist.

With blinding speed Joe's hand flashed up into a hard back fist across his temple. Fil gasped and staggered back.

"Stop!" The center referee screamed. "Point?'

The three corner judges and the center ref pointed to Joe. One nothing.

The crowd roared. Fil was angry. He had fallen for one of the oldest tricks in the book. It wouldn't happen again.

"Center up!" The referee started them again. They circled each other looking for an opening.

Joe threw a flurry of kicks, but Fil was moving with each one. His dad had taught him how to be just out of reach and he was always just a hairbreadth away.

Fil stepped on the line and the referee warned him to stay in bounds. Fil looked down to see where the line was and Joe took advantage of it. He drove a vicious sidekick hard and straight into Fil's stomach.

Fil had just caught it coming in and managed a weak Kiaaa! The kick had taken some of his air, but not all. He had a "sick" belly but he would survive.

The crowd was getting into it now. They had seen two cheap shots and wanted Joe disqualified. The referees ignored them.

Again they took the line.

At the command Joe threw a flying front kick at Fil's head. If it had connected, he would of cold cocked him. Fil slid to the side and landed a hard ridge hand across Joe's stomach. It felt like he hit a plank of wood.

All four judges awarded Fil the point.

Again they centered up. At the command they both moved forward throwing punches.

The defense of both fighters brought the crowd roaring to their feet.

Joe threw a quasi haymaker giving Fil the opening he needed to score with a back fist to the side of his head.

Tied up two to two.

They centered up again and both moved at the command.

Moving in, Fil blocked a hard front kick with a "chicken wing" and spun into a compact wheel kick catching Joe in the ribcage.

Three to two. Fil was up.

Jow scored the next point with a beautiful spin kick to the stomach. Fil couldn't block it, it was as good of a kick he had ever seen, but he was able to kiaaa and tighten up enough to blunt the blow.

Tied up.

Again the referee started them. The crowd was going insane. Fil could barely hear them. He was concentrating solely on Joe.

Joe threw a hard combination combining punches and kicks forcing Fil back.

Fil was stepping on the line again and the referee called a halt to the action.

"You step out again, you lose a point." He warned.

The match started again and they met in the middle. The referee called "clash" and started to separate the two. Fil relaxed and stepped back. He let his arms drop and was astounded to see Joe cock his leg and throw a blinding fast sidekick. It caught Fil in the gut and doubled him over.

He was bent over, hands holding his stomach; tear streaming from his eyes and gasping for breath.

The referee had jumped between the two to keep Joe from throwing another technique.

The four judges held a conference and came back to issue a warning to Joe for hitting after the referee called a halt to action.

Master Cain jumped in and loudly proclaimed his protestations. He claimed there was no halt, but a call of clash.

Again the judges held a conference and rescinded the warning.

"Protect yourself at all times!"

Reminded the center referee and awarded Joe a point. Four to three, Fil was down.

The fighters went at each other again. Very little control and blinding speed was a mix that sent electricity throughout the venue.

"Point!" Screamed one of the corner judges. They didn't all agree, but enough pointed Fil's way to award him the point

"All tied up. Sudden death. Next point wins it!" The referee centered them but the scorekeeper called to him for a clarification of points.

"Relax men. I'll be right back."

Fil took the time to look around the gym. His father and Master Brown was standing side by side. His dad gave him thumbs up and Master Brown pumped his fist.

He looked around at the frenzied crowd and realized that they were cheering for him. What a rush.

Joe was looking at his instructor and gave him a barely perceptible nod. He stepped across the line and gave Fil a hard shove.

Fil didn't go down, but took several steps to regain his balance. Unfortunately, he lost his cool.

He made a giant leap and took a mighty swing at Joe. He was so angry he lost all control. He held nothing back. All his strength, all his power, all his speed and all of frustration was manifested in that punch.

The crowd roared , he missed.

Joe easily ducked under the swing and shoved him off balance. Fil fell to the floor.

The referee and other three judges separated the combatants walking them away from each other. They delivered each to the custody of their masters and again went into a conference.

Fil stood between his father and his master. Although neither spoke, he could feel their disapproval emanating from them.

The conference over, the center judge called the two over.

"This is undoubtedly one of the most dishonorable and unrespectable bouts I've ever witnessed." He said. He turned to Fil and said "you are disqualified!"

He turned and raised Joe's hand up. The crowd answered with loud boos and some threw water bottles to the floor to show their contempt.

Facing the referee he bowed. Facing Joe he did the same bow as Joe. Each barely nodded their heads.

The judges lined them up and passed out the awards then dismissed them.

Fil looked at his second place trophy. He knew that in a normal situation he would have been estatic. At this moment all he felt was shame.

Most of the boys in the division gathered around him and commiserated with him.

He tried to smile and again told them what a nice job they had all done, but the smile never reached his eyes.

He looked across the room and locked eyes with Joe. Bile rose in his throat as Joe smirked and turned away.

CHAPTER THIRTEEN

The ride home was uncomfortable. His father was driving and Master Brown rode shotgun. Fil was sitting in the middle of the back seat.

Fil sat staring at his hands, miserable. He had let everyone down, his father, Master Brown, himself, and worse of all, God.

"I owe you both an apology." Fil said. These were the first words spoken from any of them since the match.

Master Brown turned sideways in his seat so he could look at Fil.

"Why?" He asked.

"I let you down." He mumbled

"Why?" Major Brown asked again. "Because you lost?"

"No sir. I fought the best I could. I owe you apologies because I dishonored you."

Fil looked Major fully in the eyes. "It'll never happen again.

Carl Hooper interrupted. "How can you be sure?"

"Dad…It was terrible I dishonored our school, but what I did was more despicable then that." Fil paused and swallowed the lump in his throat. "I lost my witness."

Carl Hooper and Major Brown looked across at each other.

"Tell me Fil, what do you mean by that?" Asked his dad.

"I'm human. Being human means I will make mistakes. Getting mad and going after Joe was wrong. I'm also a Christian and I lost my witness in front of a thousand people. That is what hurts me. I'm going to pray for the strength to never do that again."

Again Carl Hooper and Major Brown's eyes met. They both smiled the tension seemed to dissipate.

"You've learned a lesson, neither your father nor I could of taught you." Again he faced Fil. "You can be the best at anything in the world but without God, you are nothing."

Master Brown smiled at Fil. "That realization just made you a champion in our eyes and in Gods." "Congratulations!" Said Carl Hooper.

CHAPTER FOURTEEN

School was finally in.

Fil was happy. He was starting his junior year and his whole life was great, He hated to lose, but he was over last week's tournament.

The lessons he learned and the respect he had earned from his father and Master Brown was the epitome of his fledgling career.

His mother had been proud of his second place finish, but horrified that his friendship with Joe had eroded so badly.

He had talked to Kristy earlier and she had agreed to a burger and movie this evening. Life was good.

Lunchtime was surreal. It was the first time he could remember he ate lunch without Joe.

He had seen him in a couple of his classes, but neither had taken the first step of friendship.

A lot of the male students looked at Joe and were puzzled. They knew that some kind of fundamental change had occurred, but they weren't sure what it was.

Perhaps later on he would make an overture of friendship to him. God would want him too.

He bowed his head and thanked he Lord for his meal. An excited sophomore interrupted him.

"Fil, you better get to the parking lot. Your buddy Joe is getting ready to fight Stink!"

Fil sighed. Maybe Joe needs a lesson like this to humble him. First day back. It's going to be a rough year for Joe if he gets Link Smith on his back.

Yeah right. Who was he kidding? Joe didn't want him around and Fil's feelings had been hurt, but Joe is still his friend. He shoved his tray away and headed to the parking lot.

By the time he arrived it was over. Big link Smith was lying on the ground, semi conscious and leaking blood from both nostrils. One eye was already swelled shut.

Joe was standing over him, hands clenched into fists and eyes indolently surveying the crowd. Whatever he saw satisfied him and he turned to leave, then he spotted Fil.

They stared long and hard at each other. Joe shrugged and walked away. Fil knew that there was a new bully in town.

The crowd was breaking up and Fil went to Smith and helped him up.

He handed him a handkerchief to clean his face.

"Why are you helping me?" He asked. "You don't owe me anything?"

"I told you last spring I wanted to be your friend." Said Fil.

"I don't need your help."

"No." Agreed Fil.

"I don't need anyone's help."

"No." Agreed Fil.

"I've always picked on you." Link was puzzled. "You should be glad that your buddy did this."

"I'm not."

"Why not?"

"I'm a Christian."

"So?"

"C'mon Link. Let's take a walk and let me tell you about Christ." He paused. "How about it?"

Link Smith was puzzled. First he got totally whipped by a ...a... nerd, then a former patsy wanted to talk to him? Willingly?

"Sure." He said. "Maybe it is time I listened."